YASMIN'S HAMMER

BY ANN MALASPINA

ILLUSTRATED BY DOUG CHAYKA

LEE & LOW BOOKS INC.

New York

ACKNOWLEDGMENTS

Thank-you to the following people for their expertise on Bangladesh and the Bangla language: Tanuj Malik, Bengali translator; Saleh Chowdhury, Bengali translator; Naira Khan, Lecturer, Department of Linguistics, University of Dhaka; Sreemati Mukherjee, Lecturer, Bengali Language, Department of Asian Studies, Cornell University; Golam (Sujan) Rabbany, Director, Nari Jibon Development Foundation; and Dr. Feroza Yasmin, Chairperson, Department of Linguistics, University of Dhaka. Thanks to UNICEF-Bangladesh for its work on child labor and education, and the BBC and Child Workers in Asia for their research on young brick chippers in Bangladesh. And special appreciation to my dedicated editor, Emily Hazel.—A.M.

AUTHOR'S SOURCES

Banerji, Chitrita. *Bengali Cooking: Seasons and Festivals.* London: Serif Publishing, 1997.

Bennett, Nicki. "Climate Migration," On the Ground. *New York Times*, March 23, 2008. http://kristof.blogs.nytimes.com.

Cameron, Sara. "Bangladesh: Basic Education for Hard to Reach Urban Children." UK Department of International Development/UNICEF, 2001. http://www.ucl.ac.uk.

Chatterjee, Patralekha. "Bangladesh: Schoolgirls Hold Power & Promise." The World Bank: Development 360. http://dev360.worldbank.org.

International Labour Organization. "Child Labour and Responses in South Asia: Bangladesh," 2004. http://www.ilo.org.

Noble, Ruby Q. "Listening to Girl Brick Chippers from Bangladesh." *Child Workers in Asia* newsletter, vol. 16, no. 2 (May–August 2000).

Parker, David L. *Stolen Dreams: Portraits of Working Children.* Minneapolis, MN: Lerner Publications, 1997.

Phillips, Douglas A., and Charles F. Gritzner. *Bangladesh* (Modern World Nations series). New York: Chelsea House, 2007.

UNICEF: Bangladesh. "Hammers and homework: Educating child workers in Bangladesh," Girls' Education Campaigns: Real Lives. http://www.unicef.org.

Walsh, Fergus. "The brick chippers of Dhaka." BBC News, Nov. 7, 2005. http://news.bbc.co.uk.

The World Bank: Poverty Reduction and Economic Management Sector Unit, South Asia Region. "Poverty in Bangladesh: Building on Progress," 2002. http://www.worldbank.org.

LEE & LOW BOOKS Inc., 95 Madison Avenue, New York, NY 10016
leeandlow.com

Printed in Singapore by Tien Wah Press, February 2010

Book design by Christy Hale
Book production by The Kids at Our House

The text is set in Octavian
The illustrations are rendered in oil

10   9   8   7   6   5   4   3   2   1
First Edition

Library of Congress Cataloging-in-Publication Data
Malaspina, Ann.
Yasmin's hammer / by Ann Malaspina ; illustrated by Doug Chayka. — 1st ed.
p. cm.
Summary: In Dhaka, Bangladesh, as two girls work hard all day to help support their family by chipping bricks into small pieces, older sister Yasmin seeks a way to attend school and learn to read so that she can have a better life one day. Includes author's note about conditions in Bangladesh, child labor, and how to help. Includes bibliographical references.
ISBN 978-1-60060-359-4 (hardcover : alk. paper)
[1. Child labor—Fiction. 2. Education—Fiction. 3. Family life—Bangladesh—Fiction.
4. Dhaka (Bangladesh)—Fiction. 5. Bangladesh—Fiction.] I. Chayka, Doug, ill. II. Title.
PZ7.M28955Yas 2010
[E]—dc22   2009028529

To Sabina and Rupchan, young brick chippers in Dhaka,
who inspired my story—A.M.

For my parents—D.C.

Before the sun climbs into the sky
I jump into Abba's rented rickshaw,
my hammer in one hand,
my sister, Mita, by my side.
In my lap is a box
full of Amma's tasty *khichuri*.
I breathe in the spicy smells of rice and lentils
as we start off to work.

Abba pedals through crowded Dhaka streets
in the rattling rickshaw
painted with the brightest stars,
the bluest peacock,
and a brave bandit queen from the movies.
"One day this rickshaw
will be ours," Abba promises,
pumping his legs, breathing hard.

A girl with a book bag runs in front of us.
"Look out!" I shout.
The rickshaw swerves.
I watch the girl hurry across the street.
"Tomorrow may I go to school?" I ask.
"Not yet, Yasmin. Maybe next year," Abba says.
"We need your help now.
I must pay for the rickshaw,
and Amma's rice bag is empty again."
"Soon," I whisper to myself.

Every morning as Abba jingles the rickshaw bell,
I watch Dhaka fly by.
What a tall city—
so different from the village
where we used to live.
Stacks of jute sacks filled with fragrant rice.
Mounds of clay pots and plastic plates.
Towers of sour limes as high as palm trees.

What a loud city!
The call to prayer rings out
from a thousand mosques.
Baby taxis beep their horns.
Merchants shout to customers:
"Mustard!" "Green coconuts!"
Beggars cry out for *taka* coins.
Everywhere, black crows caw.

Once we lived far away
in a quiet house by a lazy river.
I helped Abba plant rice in the paddy field.
Amma wove baskets to sell at the market,
and Mita played under the mango tree.
Sometimes I rode our *mohish*
in the warm river currents.
The gentle water buffalo
took me to the far shore.

That was before the cyclone
crashed in from the sea.
Before the wind cried so loud,
we had to cover our ears.
Before the rain fell so hard,
Abba had to hold on to Mita
so she wouldn't be swept away
like Abba's tender new rice,
our bamboo house,
and the mango tree.
That was before water covered
our whole world.

"Good-bye! Good-bye!"
we told our cousins
who stayed behind
to rebuild their houses.
"Feed our mohish for us," Abba said.
Then we walked for many days
all the way to Dhaka
carrying Amma's baskets,
our dreams,
and nothing else.
"In the city we can begin a new life,"
Abba promised.

In Dhaka now I see words everywhere.
Signs flashing. Men waving newspapers.
And every day we pass the store
that is bursting with books.
How can I know what the words say
if I cannot read? I wonder.

Abba's feet spin the pedals
until we reach the brickyard
where workers swing their hammers,
chipping mountains of bricks
into heaps of broken pieces
to build the rickshaw roads
and sky-high buildings of Dhaka.

We say good-bye to Abba.
He must hurry away
to find paying customers.

"No time to waste," our boss yells.
"Hurry! You're too slow."
While he sits in the shade doing nothing,
Mita and I crouch on the ground.
We swing our hammers—
chipping, cracking,
crushing, smashing.
Bricks fly into bits.
Red dust fills the air
and sticks in my throat.
I spit out the grit in my mouth
and rub the ache in my shoulder.
"Work!" the boss tells us.
"Don't be lazy."

My arm is tired
but I keep swinging my hammer.
If I could read, I think,
I would not break another brick
or wash a rich lady's laundry like Amma
or pedal a rickshaw through crowded streets.
If I could read, I could be a shopkeeper
or maybe a teacher. I could be a doctor
or even the governor!
I could be anything at all.

"Quit daydreaming!" the boss yells.
"Work! Work!"
Mita strikes a brick with her hammer,
forgetting to look.
"Ouch!" she cries.
Her thumb turns red and starts to swell.
"Be brave, Mita," I tell her. "Don't stop yet.
Soon it will be time to go home."

At night Amma wraps Mita's thumb
in a clean cloth.
I see the worry in Amma's eyes.
"You must be more careful," she says.

"What did you do today, Amma?" I ask.
"Ironing. Sweeping. Washing dishes."
Amma yawns. "Someday, Yasmin,
you will work in a fine house too."
"But I don't want to sweep
a rich lady's floor," I say.
"I want to go to school.
I must learn to read, or else . . ."
Amma wrinkles her forehead.
"We want you to go too, Yasmin.
But not yet. We still need you
to work at the brickyard," Amma says.
"The *borsha* rains are coming.
The money you earn will help
Abba buy supplies
to fix our leaky roof and keep us dry."

"Soon," I whisper to myself,
because now I have a plan.

The next day at the brickyard,
crouching in the hot sun,
I swing my hammer extra hard.
I break more bricks than anyone else.
"Good girl," the boss says,
and slips extra taka coins into my hand.

Each day I pound harder, faster.
Bricks fly into bits. Red dust fills the air.
I cough. My shoulders ache.
But little by little my pile of coins grows.

At night I hide the coins under our bed.
When I sleep, I dream of many things:
our mohish in the river,
Abba's green rice paddy,
and a pile of books.

Many days later,
on our way to the brickyard,
I tell Abba, "Don't wait for us tonight.
We will walk home."
"Good," says Abba.
"I can pick up more customers.
Be careful crossing the busy streets."

After work I try to remember
the way back—up this street
and down that one.
"Are we lost?" Mita asks.
The cars and buses beep so loud,
I forget which turns to take.
My heart pounds.

I see the flashing signs
and the men waving newspapers.
At last I find the store
that is bursting with books.
So many books.
How will I choose just one?

"Can you read?" the shopkeeper asks,
staring down at me.
I shake my head no.
He pulls a book from a high shelf.
"This is the one for you," he says.
I spread my coins on the table.
The shopkeeper counts twice.
"Is that all you have?"
I nod. He wraps the book in paper
and slips Mita a sweet.
I thank him and hold the book close.

By the time we reach home,
we are out of breath from running
and the sun is low in the sky.
Abba is fixing the roof.
"Abba, come see!" I call. He puts the nails
in his pocket and climbs down.

Inside, Amma has chopped a fat pumpkin
and an onion. She is making curry.
"Amma, look what I have!" I say.
She wipes her hands.
Just then our only lightbulb
blinks off. Another power cut.
Amma lights a candle.

Carefully, I open the book.
Each page has a picture
with a word below it.
There is a dinghy,
and a rice paddy,
and an elephant.
Everyone leans in to look.

"Once I heard a *bagh* growling
in the forest," Abba says,
pointing to the picture of a tiger.
Amma turns the page
and traces the pretty petals
of a white water lily.
"*Shapla*," she murmurs.
I think of the water lilies floating
on the faraway river
we once lived beside.
We look at the pictures,
remembering together.
But then we are quiet.
None of us can read the words.

Suddenly Abba stands up.
The flame shivers. "The girls
must go to school," he says.
This time Amma does not say,
"Not yet," or "Maybe next year."
This time she says, "Soon.
They must go soon."

Long after I'm in bed,
I hear their voices.
Abba and Amma
are whispering, planning.
I close my eyes,
hoping, dreaming.
"Soon," I whisper to myself.
"Very soon."

Abba finds a second rickshaw route
with more paying customers.
In the evenings, after Amma sweeps
and scrubs all day, she weaves
baskets to sell at the market.
When Amma comes home one afternoon,
I see a box of brand-new pencils
in her shopping bag.

And every day Mita and I swing
our hammers as fast as we can—
chipping, cracking,
crushing, smashing—
eager for more taka coins.

One morning I jump into Abba's rickshaw,
my hammer in one hand,
a box of warm khichuri in my lap,
and Mita by my side.
We pass the towers of limes and coconuts,
stacks of jute sacks, and flashing signs.

Abba turns down a strange road.
Mita and I hold on tight
as the rickshaw rattles and sways.
The brickyard is the other way.
"Where are we going, Abba? We'll be late!"
Abba pedals harder. I see him smile.

Then I know.
This is the way to school.

BANGLADESH

Afterword

The People's Republic of Bangladesh is a small South Asian country located on the Bay of Bengal—the northern part of the Indian Ocean. With a fast-growing population, Bangladesh is one of the most crowded nations in the world. In the past the majority of Bangladeshis were farmers. Now more and more people are leaving their rural villages and moving to the capital, Dhaka. Some people flee cyclones, the powerful storms that flood the low-lying country. Cyclones often wash away fields of rice, jute, and other crops. The high winds and heavy rainfall destroy houses as well, leaving many people homeless. In Dhaka, people can find jobs in factories, mills, shops, and small businesses.

The economy is developing, but nearly half of all Bangladeshis still live in poverty. Sometimes children need to work to help support their families. The children take low-paying jobs as tea servers, housemaids, rag collectors, street sweepers, or matchbox makers. Some children work as brick chippers, using hammers to break bricks made of baked clay. The crumbled bricks are mixed with cement to form concrete, which is used to construct buildings and to pave roads throughout the country.

Although it is not always easy for families to send their children to school, people in Bangladesh recognize that education is the best way to end poverty. The government is working to end child labor and to provide affordable schooling for children. Several national and international aid and human rights organizations, such as the Bangladesh Rehabilitation Assistance Committee and Save the Children, are also working to make education a reality for all the children of Bangladesh.

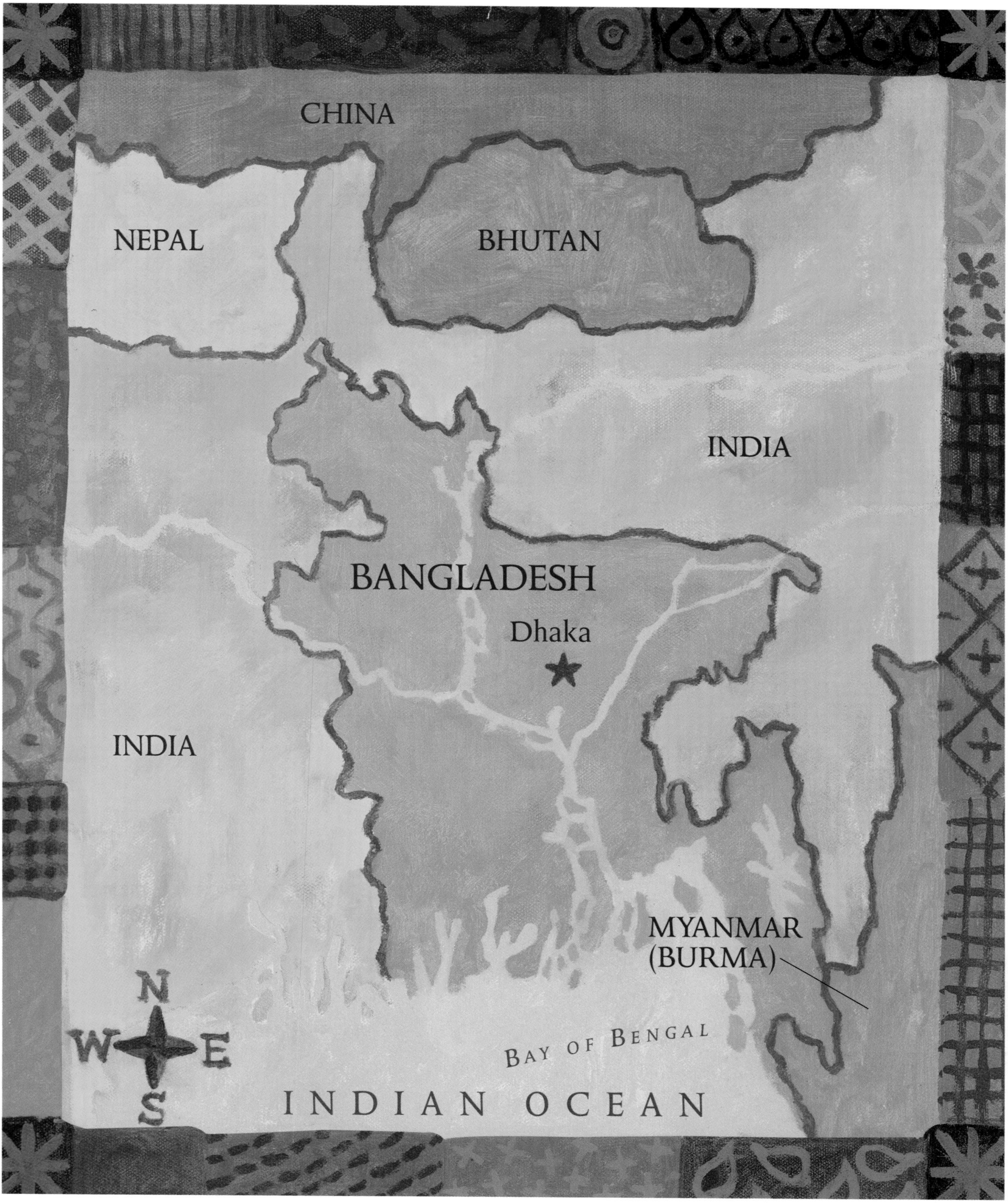

CHINA

NEPAL

BHUTAN

INDIA

BANGLADESH

Dhaka
★

INDIA

MYANMAR
(BURMA)

N
W E
S

BAY OF BENGAL

INDIAN OCEAN

How You Can Help

For more information about what is being done to help children in Bangladesh and other parts of the world, and to learn how you can support these efforts, please visit the following organizations online.

Bangladesh Rehabilitation Assistance Committee (BRAC) works to alleviate poverty and empower the poor through economic development, health care, education, human rights protection, and legal services. www.brac.net

Global Movement for Children (GMC) is a worldwide network of people and organizations working to improve the lives of children, largely focusing on poverty, child labor, and education. www.gmfc.org

Save the Children, an international aid organization, is partnered with groups in Bangladesh to end child labor and protect children's rights. www.savethechildren.net/alliance

United Nations Children's Fund (UNICEF) aims to protect and provide for the basic needs of at-risk children, including victims of war, disasters, poverty, violence, and those with disabilities. www.supportunicef.org

Further Reading

Howard, Ginger. *A Basket of Bangles*. Brookfield, CT: Millbrook Press, 2002.

Orr, Tamra B. *Bangladesh* (Enchantment of the World series). Danbury, CT: Children's Press, 2007.

Perkins, Mitali. *Rickshaw Girl*. Watertown, MA: Charlesbridge Publishing, 2007.

Rahman, Urmi. *B is for Bangladesh*. London: Frances Lincoln Children's Books, 2009.

Thomson, Ruth. *Living in Bangladesh*. New York: Franklin Watts, 2005.

Glossary and Pronunciation Guide

The following entries include Bangla names and words, which have been adapted for spoken English. Some variations in spelling and pronunciation may exist.

Abba (ah-BAH): father

Amma (ah-MAH): mother

baby taxi: motorized three-wheeled vehicle

bagh (bahgh): tiger

bamboo (bam-BOO): treelike tropical plant with a hard, hollow stem, used for building homes and furniture

Bangladesh (BAHNG-lah-desh *or* bahng-lah-DESH): South Asian country bordered by India, Myanmar (Burma), and the Bay of Bengal

borsha (bor-SHAH): summer rainy season

call to prayer: announcement that summons Muslims to prayer five times a day

cyclone (SYE-klohn): severe tropical storm

Dhaka (DHA-kah): capital of Bangladesh

dinghy (DING-ee): small boat

jute (joot): plant with strong fibers used to make rope, sacks, and mats

khichuri (KI-choor-ee): spicy dish made of rice and lentils

Mita (MEE-tah): girl's name

mohish (moh-HISH): water buffalo

mosque (mosk): Muslim place of worship

rickshaw (RIK-shah *or* RIK-shaw): cartlike passenger vehicle pulled by a bicycle

shapla (SHAHP-lah): water lily

taka (TAH-kah): money used in Bangladesh

Yasmin (YAHS-min): girl's name